A TALE OF TAILS

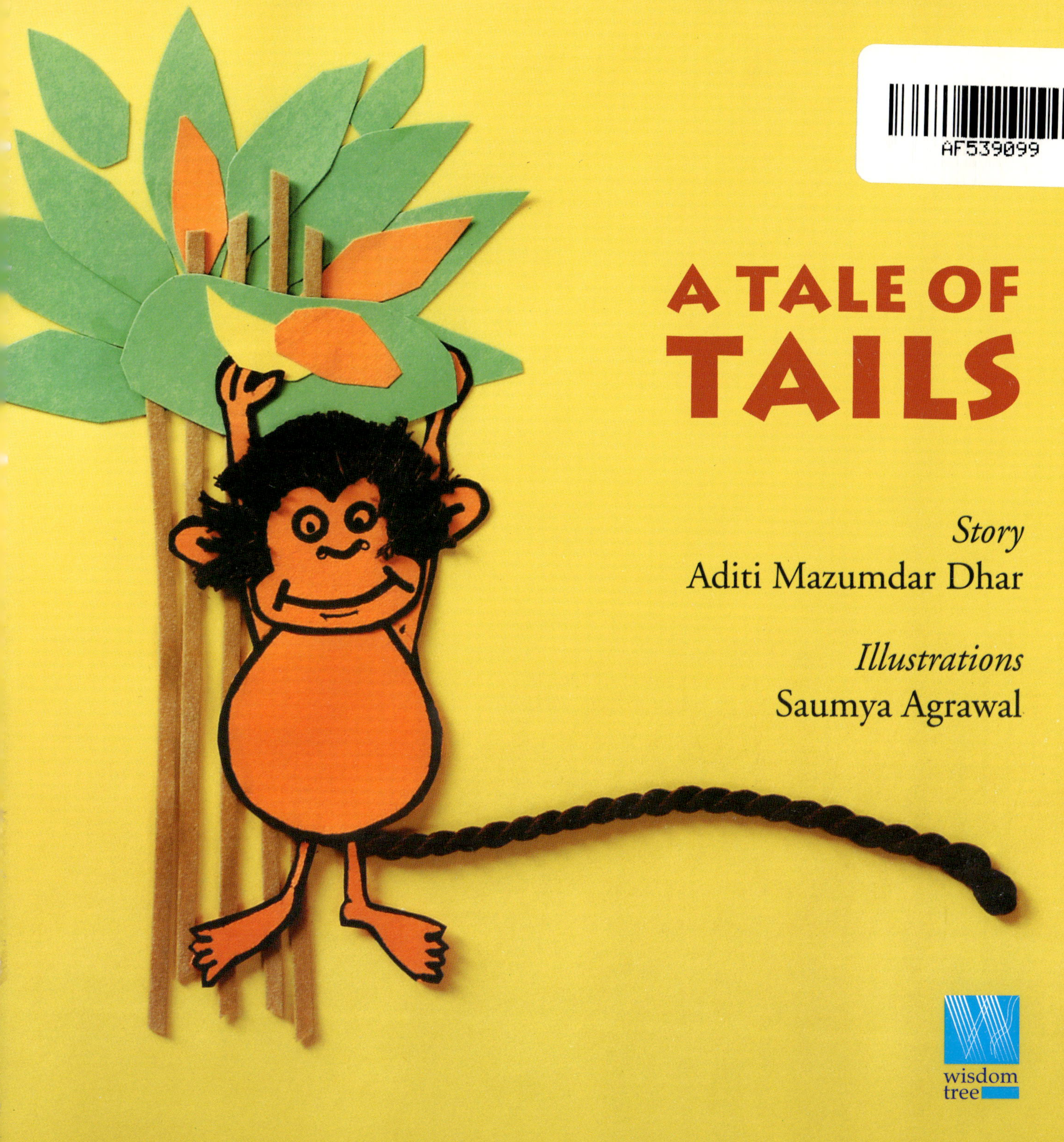

Story
Aditi Mazumdar Dhar

Illustrations
Saumya Agrawal

wisdom tree

Simi and her kid brother Toto lived in a small town in India.

One day both Simi & Toto were cribbing. Grown-ups had so much fun! No one scolds or stops them from doing what they want. How they wished they could be like the grown-ups!

Hand-in-hand, the brother and sister strolled towards the jungle. They walked and walked till they were deep in the jungle and were really tired.

As they settled down under the shade of a large tree, the jungle suddenly came to life and a whole new story book opened out in front of them.

They heard a LOUD noise. It seemed as if a large number of animals were marching together. Yes! Indeed they were. Different animals gathered together in the clearing where the children were seated, as if for a meeting. There were zebras, squirrels, monkeys, giraffes, rabbits, tigers, lions and birds of different types. BUT... wait! There was something very strange about them all.

Simi and Toto crept in closer for a better look and what they saw made them roll with silent laughter. *None of the animals had their own tails*! The children stared in amazement when they saw a leopard with a fish's tail...

and a zebra with a peacock's tail, all very bright and fancy. He was tapping his hooves as if getting ready to do the rain-dance!

and *imagine*...Jumbo, the elephant with a tiger's tail which kept getting entangled between his legs. Poor Jumbo could not even sweep the flies away.

All the animals looked upset and were grumbling. The king of the jungle, who had a fluffy squirrel's tail, roared loudly, "*Quiet*!" The jungle settled into silence instantly. The lion said, "Hope all of you enjoyed exchanging your tails."

"Oh no! Lord. We have had the most terrible time over the past three days," said the rabbit that sported a monkey's tail.

"Why? You all wanted each other's tails, so I asked God for this boon," said their king.

EEEEEEEEEAAAAAAAAAAAAOOO! The wise elephant wagged his tiger tail and said, "Sir, the tail of every animal is useful to him in some special way. The monkey's tail helps him hang and swing from tree to tree while the fish uses its tail to swim."

The tiger said, "I use my tail to balance myself when I run after my prey. I haven't been able to hunt in the last three days at all. I am *so hungry."*

CCCAAAAAAAAAWWWW said the peacock, "My colourful tail helps me to attract the peahens."

All the animals complained about their new-found tails and at last, the old lion king roared, "Let's just get back our tails and be happy with the gift of Nature."

Now Simi and Toto understood that it is better to be happy with what we are rather than try to be somebody else.

Activities

Spot six differences in the two pictures.

Match the animals with their tails

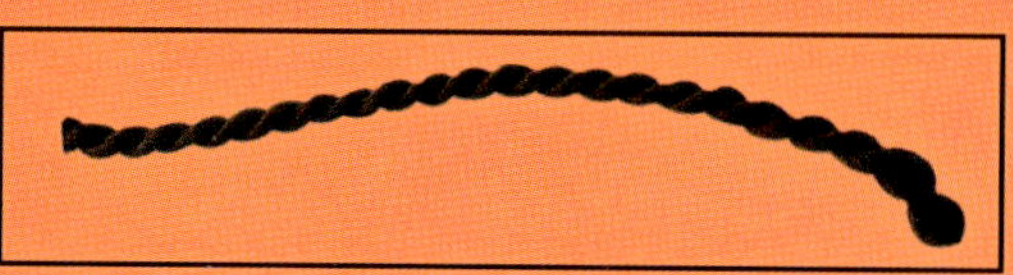

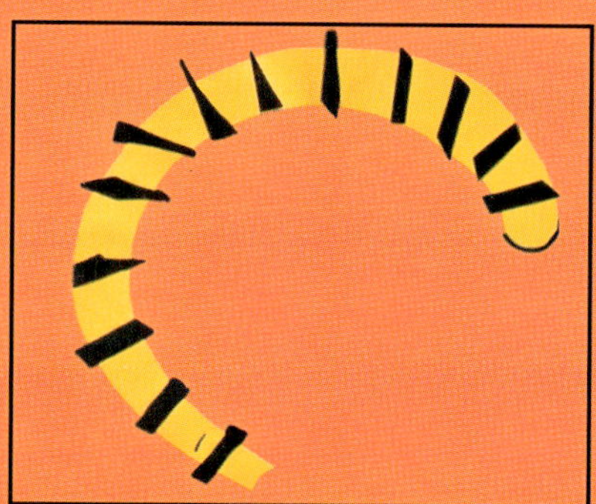

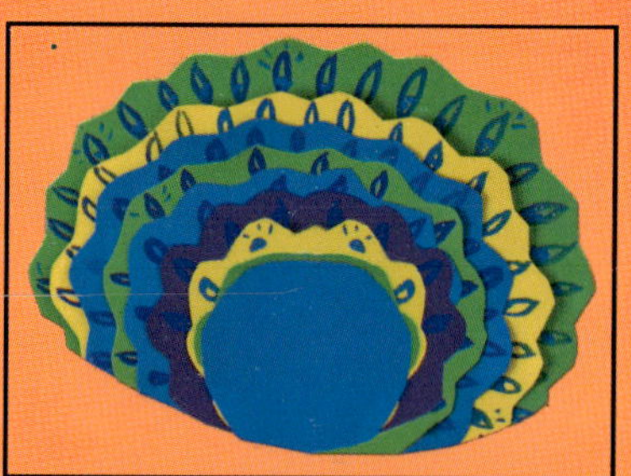